SPY

RC

Made with ♥ on the Notion Press Platform
www.notionpress.com

I would Like to dedicate this book to my love, my heart, my RADHA, MY everything can't take her name....

and also to my Friend, my blood, Venki

Also by the grace of Shri RADHAKRISHN i am writing actually they are....

also along comes my parents' efforts, no one can measure their pain, some are natural but many are mine given....

Lastly, I would like to thank me for doing this for them....

Contents

Contents

Foreword

Welcome to the world of espionage, where secrets, lies, and danger are the norm. In this book, you will be taken on a journey through the thrilling and complex world of spies.

Espionage has been a part of human history for centuries, and has evolved in tandem with advancements in technology and political systems. From ancient civilizations to modern-day intelligence agencies, the art of spying has played a crucial role in shaping the course of history.

This book explores the various aspects of espionage, including the tools and techniques used by spies, the different types of intelligence gathering, and the strategies employed in covert operations. Through the pages of this book, you will gain a deeper understanding of the clandestine world of spying, and the men and women who risk their lives to protect their countries and interests.

So buckle up, get ready to be immersed in the fascinating world of espionage and let us delve into the secret world of spies.

Preface

I have always been fascinated by the world of spies and espionage. The idea of secret agents, covert operations, and international intrigue captured my imagination from an early age. As I grew older, my interest in the subject only deepened, and I found myself devouring books, articles, and movies related to the world of espionage.

Over the years, I realized that while there are numerous books and articles on the subject of espionage, there are very few that offer a comprehensive overview of the field. As a result, I decided to write this book - a comprehensive guide to the world of spies, covering everything from the history of espionage to the tools and techniques used by modern-day intelligence agencies.

The aim of this book is to provide readers with a detailed understanding of the fascinating and complex world of espionage. Drawing on my extensive research and personal experience, I have tried to create a book that is both informative and entertaining.

This book is intended for anyone who is interested in the subject of espionage, whether they are seasoned professionals, students of the field, or simply casual readers looking for an exciting and informative read. I hope that this book will not only provide readers with a deeper understanding of the world of spies, but also inspire them to think critically about the role of intelligence gathering in modern society.

I am grateful to all those who have supported me in writing this book, and I hope that readers will find it to be a valuable addition to their libraries.

Radhe Radhe

Thank you for reading.
RC

Acknowledgements

Writing a book is not a solitary endeavor, and I am grateful to the many people who have supported me throughout this journey. I would like to take this opportunity to express my heartfelt gratitude to the following individuals and organizations:

First and foremost, I would like to thank my family for their unwavering support and encouragement. Their love and understanding have been a constant source of strength and inspiration.

I would also like to express my gratitude to my friends and colleagues, who have offered their valuable insights and feedback throughout the writing process. Their constructive criticism and encouragement have been invaluable in helping me to refine my ideas and improve the quality of this book.

I am indebted to the many experts in the field of espionage, whose books, articles, and interviews have provided me with the knowledge and inspiration to write this book. I would also like to acknowledge the countless individuals who have dedicated their lives to the world of intelligence gathering, often at great personal risk.

I would like to extend a special thanks to my editor and the publishing team, who have worked tirelessly to ensure the success of this book. Their professionalism and expertise have been instrumental in bringing this project to fruition.

Finally, I would like to thank the readers of this book, whose interest and support have made it all possible. It is my sincere hope that this book will provide you with a deeper understanding of the world of espionage, and inspire you to think critically about the role of intelligence gathering in modern society.

Prologue

The air was thick with smoke and the acrid smell of burning metal. In the distance, explosions echoed through the night, sending shockwaves through the ground. The sky was a deep shade of orange, the color of flames and destruction.

Amidst the chaos, a figure moved swiftly, darting between the burning wreckage of buildings and vehicles. He wore a dark cloak that billowed in the wind, and his face was obscured by a hood. He moved with purpose, his steps sure and confident despite the danger that surrounded him.

As he approached a massive, fortified building, he paused, scanning the area for any signs of danger. Satisfied that he was alone, he stepped forward and placed his hand on the door. With a sudden burst of energy, he sent a wave of force through the metal, shattering the lock and sending the door flying off its hinges.

Without hesitation, he stepped inside, and the door slammed shut behind him. He was surrounded by darkness, but his eyes quickly adjusted, revealing a vast, cavernous space filled with machines, screens, and complex equipment. This was the heart of the operation, the place where the fate of the world would be decided.

He took a deep breath and closed his eyes, focusing his mind on the task at hand. He had come too far, risked too much, to fail now. With a surge of power, he began to work, his fingers moving deftly over the keyboard as he accessed the system.

This was it. The moment he had been waiting for, the chance to make a difference in the world. As he worked, he knew that there would be no turning back. He had chosen his path, and he was ready to face whatever lay ahead.

The fate of the world hung in the balance, and he was the only one who could save it.

CHAPTER I

The Assignment

Jack worked for the top-secret government entity known only as "The Agency."He had built a reputation as a master of disguise and espionage, with a keen eye for detail and a cunning wit that allowed him to blend into any situation with ease. With his sharp features and piercing blue eyes, he cut an imposing figure, but he was also charming and confident, a deadly combination that made him one of the most sought-after agents in the business.

On a hot summer day, Jack was summoned to the agency's headquarters for a briefing on his next mission. The edifice was an enormous structure in the middle of the city, with its entry identified only by an inconspicuous sign and a security checkpoint guarded by armed guards. He drew a deep breath as he approached, feeling a tingle of exhilaration at the prospect of the danger that lied ahead.

The headquarters was a maze of winding halls and offices, with photos of past directors and agents who had established a name for themselves in the field adorning the walls. Jack walked through the maze-like corridors, his shoes reverberating off the smooth marble surface. He entered his boss's office, a majestic space with a massive mahogany desk and floor-to-ceiling windows with a stunning view of the city.

His employer, a man renowned for his exquisite taste and no-nonsense approach, sat behind the desk, scrutinising a file. As Jack entered the room, he looked up and motioned for him to take a seat.

"Jack, thank you for arriving on such short notice," his supervisor remarked solemnly.

"I have received information that a criminal organisation known as the Shadow Syndicate is plotting a huge attack on our country. This gang is very sophisticated and works in the shadows, making gathering useful intelligence on their actions challenging. That's where you come into play."

Jack listened closely, his mind spinning with ideas of what this mission may involve. He was no stranger to danger, and he was well aware of the hazards involved, but he was a professional with a responsibility to safeguard his country and its people.

"I understand, sir," Jack answered. "What do you require of me?"

"We need you to infiltrate the Shadow Syndicate and collect as much information as possible," his supervisor remarked. "We suspect they have a mole within the agency, which is why we need someone with your talents to handle this."

Jack nodded, a giddy feeling developing within him. This was a high-stakes operation that would put his training and ability to the test. He was, however, up for the challenge.

"I'll do all in my ability to fulfil this assignment successfully, sir," Jack stated emphatically.

His boss smiled, with a hint of satisfaction in his eyes. "I knew I could count on you, Jack. "You are one of our best agents, and I have no doubt that you will get the job done."

With that, Jack left the office, his mind already focused on the mission ahead. He was ready for anything that might come his way, and he had a sense of purpose that he had not felt in a long time. He was a spy, and he was proud to serve his country.

Jack spent the next few days researching the Shadow Syndicate and learning everything he could about it. He went through records and analysed intelligence, drawing up a picture of the organisation and its founders. He was keen to find whatever flaws he might exploit and get entry to the group's inner circles.

While examining his notes one evening, Jack's attention was drawn to a name he had come across numerous times before: Maria. She was a Syndicate member with a reputation as a brilliant hacker and intelligence worker. Jack couldn't ignore the impression that there was something familiar about her, so he decided to investigate more.

What he discovered surprised him. Maria was an old love, someone he had known many years before joining the organisation. They had been in love when they were young, but their careers had diverged and they had lost contact over the years.

Jack was now in a difficult situation. He had always been a professional at his job, never allowing his emotions to get in the way of a mission. But this was unique. He had a strong bond with Maria, and he was divided between his responsibilities to the agency and his desire to protect her.

He knew he couldn't allow his personal sentiments interfere with the task, but he also couldn't bear the thought of betraying someone he had once loved. For days, he agonised over the decision, divided between his allegiance to the agency and his desire to protect Maria.

Finally, he made a decision that would alter his life forever. He resolved to approach Maria, persuade her to leave the Shadow Syndicate, and urge her to assist him in bringing the organisation down from inside. It was a hazardous approach, but he thought it was the only way to finish his goal and keep Maria safe.

Jack started carrying out his plan because he was committed to seeing it through. Although he was aware that the trip would be lengthy and challenging, he was prepared for whatever lied ahead. A spy, he was also in love.

CHAPTER II

The Reunion

The top members of the Syndicate were there in the lavish ballroom, but Jack's attention was only on one of them. His pulse raced at the notion of finally meeting Maria after all these years as he pushed his way through the crowd. When he finally caught a glimpse of her, his heart began to race. She exceeded his memory of her beauty.

Their eyes were closed as they held one other close in a tight hug. As if the hug were reversing the time that had passed between them, they didn't want to release one other. When they eventually began to back away, they were beaming with happiness and grinning from ear to ear.

They took a walk in the garden, and they talked for hours. They reminisced about their time together, and they laughed at all of the silly things they used to do. They talked about their lives since they last saw each other,

"Do you remember the peon whom we tricked and laslty he was fired becasue we made him belive that all staff thought he was rude"

"yes..." "and also that when we planned a party for Marry and gifted her a small chocolate..."

"And that...."

"what...?"

"nothing..it's just ... leave it"

"comeon tell me..."

"Nothing 10 dec"

"what's thjat"

"your last day in school before your dad"s trasfer"

"you still remember....!"

they both realized how much they still cared for each other.
"How you entered here with such tight security?"
"some flips and rolls and tadaa..."
"bruu..."

The first to express his emotions was Jack, who told Maria that he had never really let go of her. She was still the love of his life, he informed her, and he yearned to spend time with her once more. Maria was surprised by his remarks, yet she couldn't help but feel her heart flutter. She said that she was still in love with him and that she had remained unchanged from him.

Jack and Maria made the most of their time together during the following several weeks. They liked each other's company, went on walks, and had in-depth discussions. Every day, their bond became deeper and they found themselves falling in love all over again.

They discussed the future and came to the conclusion that they wanted to live out the rest of their lives together. Maria joyfully accepted Jack's marriage proposal once he made it. They began preparing for their marriage, which would take place on the stunning beach where they had had their first kiss.

The day of the wedding was magnificent, radiant with love and joy. In front of their loved ones, Jack and Maria exchanged vows, and as they said "I do," they both understood that their love was indestructible.

After their nuptials, Jack and Maria went on a vacation around Europe, seeing various cities and taking in the sights. They went to the city of love, Paris, and saw the Eiffel Tower illuminated at night. They travelled to Venice and rode in a gondola around the picturesque canals of the city. They also went to Rome, where they viewed the Vatican and the Colosseum.

They went home with memories that would last a lifetime, and their love only grew deeper. They settled into married life and began to create a future that was full of love, humour, and excitement.

Jack and Maria's love only got stronger as the years went by. They encountered difficulties, but they always supported one another, their love giving them the fortitude to confront everything. They co-raised a family and watched as their kids grew up and established their own families.

Jack and Maria never lost sight of the love that brought them back together as they grew older together. They frequently discussed how their reunion was the happiest day of their life. They demonstrated to one another and to the world that genuine love never dies and can be revived and brought back to life with a little work and will. So they knew that their love story would go on forever as they held hands and watched the sun go down.

I know you also fill it is like a fairy tale and that is.... it was just dream expected to happen for future, but future was palying with some new toys......

As soon as he proposed she backed and what can to he mind, she ran away from him, ARon stands there still knowing that she have to chase with his work and love.....

CHAPTER III

A Tragedy Unfolds

Paris was illuminated by a soft glow as the sun set on the city's cobblestone streets. A light breeze carried the enticing aroma of hot croissants from a nearby bakery into the air. Marie moved across town, his heart pounding.In his enigmatic message, Henri had asked that they meet at an unidentified location. Since the communication had been concise and direct, he felt nervous and anxious.

When he arrived at the designated spot, a quiet alleyway in the heart of the city, he wondered what could be so important that Henri had to reach out to him in this manner. He would discover this shortly.

Henri was standing in the alley as he entered, with a frightened look on his face. He turned to face her, and their eyes locked. They just stood there for a long time, watching each other. It had been a while since their last meeting, and Marie had really missed him.

Henri spoke first, his voice agitated. "I need your assistance, Aaron," he said as he grasped his arm. The speaker continued, "I've been working on a secret government operation, and I've found some material that may be harmful to both of us."

Aron's heartbeat picked up. What may he have discovered to be so dangerous? He inquired, his voice quivering with fear.

"I've discovered proof of a plot to overthrow the government, and it involves some of the most powerful people in the country," Henri said.

"I need your help to put a stop to it."

The terror swept through Aron. Even though he had always known Henri was a spy, he never dreamed he would find himself in such a dangerous situation—especially one that his boss had previously mentioned. In spite of his fear, he said, "What can I do to help?"

Henri said, "I need you to gather this information and provide it to me."

Not much time is left. "We must respond fast since the tactic is already in play."

Aron nodded, becoming more determined. Since he had always known that he and Henri were meant to be together, he was grateful for their connection more than ever. They started gathering information and assembling the puzzle pieces.

Days passed, and while they made progress, their success was transient. One evening, when they convened in the alleyway to discuss their findings, they were ambushed. Men with guns stormed into the alley, shouting orders and aiming their weapons towards Henri and Aron.

Henri hid behind Aron to shield him from the danger. He took out his own gun and fired, killing two of the attackers. There were too many of them, and Henri was outnumbered. He turned to Aron and, in a last-ditch act of bravery, shouted, "Run."

Aron did not hesitate or consider his options. His heart was racing as he began to go down the alley. As he turned the corner and reached the end of the alley, he could hear bullets coming from behind him. He continued sprinting without pausing to turn around.

Henri was nowhere to be seen, and when he finally stopped to catch his breath, he screamed in fear. Has he been arrested? Had he already diedo be seen, and when he finally stopped to catch his breath, he screamed in fear.

Has he been arrested? Had he already died? He was trying to come up with a plan, and his mind was whirling with possibilities. He knew that to locate help, stop the plot, and get away before it was too late, he had to keep moving.

As he moved across the city, he had a sense of urgency. He had to find

He needed to find the firearms dealer before he could finish his next big deal. He was no closer to finding him, though, since his quest for him had come to a standstill.

He was drinking coffee while sitting at a café when he had the uneasy feeling that someone was observing him. His instincts, which he had developed through years of training, warned him of danger. He quickly glanced across the crowded room, but he failed to spot anyone who stuck out.

Then, from behind her, he heard a quiet voice. When he turned back, he saw a tall, dark-haired man standing behind her and said, "Agent BR, I have been awaiting you." His eyes were icy and penetrating, and he was wearing a well-cut suit.

He asked, attempting to keep his voice calm, "Who are you?"

He said, "My name is Jean-Luc." "And I am aware of your search criteria." "You can go to him with me."

He said, "I don't know what you're talking about; it sounds like you've had a little too much to drink."

She said, "I don't think so." "Maybe you shouldn't have met Henri."

Despite his reluctance, Aron realised he had to seize this chance. As a result, he surrenders to them as they point guns at him.

He couldn't get rid of the uneasy sensation he had as they awaited their rendezvous. In his line of business, he had dealt with many dangerous individuals, but there was something about Jean-Luc that made him uneasy.

Amelia's worries came true that evening as they travelled through Paris's winding, dark alleyways. He was ambushed by a gang of armed men after being lured into a trap by Jean-Luc.

Despite being outnumbered and outgunned, he battled valiantly. He was ultimately overcome, and while he was being battered to unconsciousness, he passed out.

He was chained and gagged as he awoke in a poorly lit room. With an evil grin, Jean-Luc was standing in front of him.

He responded, "Agent BR, you ought to have remained out of this." "This struggle was never going to be won by you." I'm not a monster, though. I'm open to working out a deal with you. "If you agree to halt your probe, I'll let you go."

Of course, BR declined. Whatever the cost, he wouldn't give up. He was then beaten again and abandoned.

He became aware that he was a piece in a far bigger game as he lay there, drifting in and out of awareness. The forces he was up against were considerably more potent than he could have anticipated, and the arms dealer was only the tip of the iceberg.

He therefore made a promise to himself. He would make his way out, and he would figure out a method to exact revenge on those who had injured her. No matter the price, he would not relent.

He couldn't help but have the sensation that this was only the start of a long and perilous trip as he fell asleep.

He was simply thankful to be alive and to have contributed to the struggle against evil. His joy, however, did not last long since one of his fellow operatives sent him a distress signal. Despite the message's ambiguity, he understood that it concerned his life or death.

In a hurry, BR grabbed his belongings and embarked on a new assignment, determined to save his fellow agent and permanently bring down the organization. This time, he was extra wary because he knew the group was aware of him and his activities.

In a hurry, BR grabbed his belongings and embarked on a new assignment, determined to save his fellow agent and permanently bring down the organization. This time, he was extra wary because he knew the group was aware of him and his activities.

He made his way to the area outside the city where he thought the spy was being held hostage. He couldn't get the notion that something wasn't right since the village was quiet—almost too quiet.

The agent was being kept in an abandoned building, and as he got closer, he saw that the windows were broken and the door was falling off its hinges. He carefully entered the structure with his pistol ready.

He could hear a struggle coming from one of the rooms as he moved through the wet, dark hallways. When the door was forced open, she was confronted by the organization's boss.

He had a sick grin on his face and was holding his fellow agent at gunpoint. He informed BR that he would have to give up the knowledge he had gained if he wanted to save his friend.

BR had to make a hard choice. He had two options: he could fight and put his friend's life in danger, or he could hand over the information and put the security of his nation at risk. He considered his choices as he tried to come up with a strategy.

Just then, the structure began to tremble, and explosions could be heard reverberating down the hallways. When BR noticed that support had at last come, he used the decoy to disarm the leader and save his companion.

When the group was ultimately defeated, Aron and his companion managed to flee the burning structure. Though startled, they were both happy to still be alive.

Aron couldn't help but reflect on the costs he had paid in the name of duty as they returned to the main office. But he also understood that he would go through it all again to protect his nation and hold those who harmed it accountable.

With the mission's conclusion, Aron's life began a new chapter, and he was prepared to confront whatever was ahead of him with courage and tenacity.

CHAPTER IV

Pain and Tears

Aron's life turned around at the mission's conclusion. But at what cost did he achieve what he set out to do?His mind was heavy with the thoughts of the people he had lost, the sacrifices he had made, and the dangers he had taken.

Because of the images from his past, he had trouble sleeping at night. He would toss and turn, reliving the terrifying, depressing, and heartbreaking times. It seemed as though the ghosts of his past were still with him, bringing back memories of what he had been through.

He found himself out and about at night, trying to get away from the memories that were choking her. He ended up in a small park, where he sat on a bench and observed the night sky. He felt a gentle hand on his shoulder as he sat there, lost in thought.

He smiled lightly as he turned to see a woman standing behind her. He said he was an Amelia and that he had trouble sleeping after returning from the war as well. He encouraged him to do the same, telling him that he had found solace in the stars.

When he felt overwhelmed by his memories, Aron took his words to heart and began gazing upward at the stars. He was able to begin healing from the wounds of his past as he slowly but surely found peace in their twinkling light.

Additionally, he began to share his experiences and emotions with his friends and family. He discovered that discussing his pain and worries helped him process them and move on.

Aron came to the realisation that, although his past would always be with her, it no longer had to define her as he continued his healing journey. He was capable of overcoming any obstacle that awaited him, and he was stronger than the memories that haunted her.

He recalled the words of the Amelia he had met in the park one night as he gazed up at the stars: "Our memories are like the stars." "Although they may pass away, they will always be a part of us." Realizing that his memories would always be with her but would no longer have to bring him pain, he smiled.

With gratitude for the journey and the lessons he had learned, Aron wiped his tears away. Knowing that he would always carry the stars of his past with him, guiding him through life's challenges, he was prepared to face the future with courage and hope.

He was lost in thought, thinking about his time as a spy and all the difficulties he had had to overcome. He had always been guided by his love for his country and his determination to make a difference, even though it had been a difficult path filled with danger and uncertainty.

Memories of the past began to flood his mind as he sat there. He thought back to the day he was first hired as a spy, the high-octane missions, the triumphs, and the close calls to losing everything. He thought, however, most of all, of the love he had lost along the way.

Despite the fact that it had been a long time since he had seen the love of his life, the memories were still as vivid as ever. Their love had been sincere and blazing since they met while they were on a mission. He had to say goodbye to the only person he had ever truly loved because, in the end, the demands of their respective jobs had broken them apart.

As he thought about all the heartache and suffering he had endured over the years, tears streamed down his cheeks. But there was a glimmer of hope in the midst of his despair. He was aware that his love had never truly died and that no matter what, it would always be there to help him overcome obstacles in life.

He also made a promise to her as he sat there and watched the sun set below the horizon. No matter what stood in his way, he would never give up on his love. He would always stand up for what was right and keep his deep-seated love alive, shining, and unwavering.

He got off the bench and left, ready to face whatever the future might bring with renewed determination. He also knew that his journey would be difficult and filled with tears, but he also knew that the love that had always guided her would never leave him.

CHAPTER V

A Day Like Any Other

He heard the crashing of the waves against the shore when he awoke. The world was bathed in a warm golden glow as the sun just began to rise above the horizon. He stretched and felt his body's muscles relax afterward.

He got dressed, put on his shoes, and went for a walk outside. His senses were energised by the cool, crisp air. He took a deep breath and enjoyed the salty air of the sea. With each step, his feet dug into the sand as he walked along the shore.

His thoughts turned to his life as a spy as he walked. He had always persevered, despite the risk and uncertainty of the journey. He had overcome numerous obstacles and prevailed each time. He was grateful for the opportunity to serve his country in such a meaningful way and was proud of everything he had accomplished.

He took in the sounds and sights of the world around him as he walked for hours. He was lost in thought, bouncing from one memory to the next, when he heard a voice all of a sudden.

"Hello, my beloved,"

He turned around, reaching for the gun on his side with one hand. He was confronted by the antagonist he had been pursuing for months. He was a master of deception and had evaded his pursuers at every turn.

He said, his evil eyes shining, "I've been waiting for this moment for a long time."

With his hand still resting on his gun, he stood firm. "What would you like?" He asked in a calm and steady voice.

"I want you to know that, as always, I am one step ahead of you. Additionally, I wish to let you know that your days as a spy are over. There is nothing you can do to prevent me from taking over your country.

He stood there silently, his face bearing a determined expression. He was an experienced spy, and he wasn't going to let this villain intimidate him.

With conviction in his voice, he declared, "You won't win."

The laughter reverberated along the shore. We'll see how that goes. Consider this a farewell greeting until then.

He then turned and vanished into the crowd, leaving him once again alone.

During that time, Aron yelled, "Best of luck and Radhe Radhe!" However, he was aware that their encounter was far from over, that he would continue to do everything in his power to stop this villain and protect his country, and that when God was on his side, there was nothing to be afraid of. He walked away as the sun set over the ocean, his mind focused on the task that lay ahead. He would do whatever it took to put an end to this villain. He would never give up, regardless of the challenges he faced.

But for the time being, he was just trying to enjoy his day. He decided to go for a walk in the park so he could get away from his life as a spy for a while and be surrounded by nature.

He enjoyed the park's sights and sounds as he walked, admiring the greenery and scent of freshly cut grass. He grinned as he observed children laughing and families playing together. He was at ease and had the impression that he was a part of something broader and more significant than just his own life.

However, as he was getting ready to leave the park and return home, he noticed something that caught his attention. On the opposite side of the park, he noticed a man who looked familiar. He felt like he had seen him before, though he was unable to identify him.

He tried to forget about it and went on his way, but he couldn't help but feel as though someone was watching him. He picked up the radio, but when he turned around, the man was still looking at him from a distance.

He quickly came to the conclusion that this was not a coincidence. He was being pursued by the man. He dove into a nearby alleyway to avoid him because he was aware that he needed to act quickly. But he was still waiting for him when he emerged on the opposite side.

When he emerged from the shadows and into the light, he was prepared to defend himself and reached for his gun. He realised who he was at that point. He had been looking for the villain for so long. the one who had wreaked so much havoc and suffered so much in his life.

He smiled slyly and said, "Hello, my dear." "It has been a while."

She tried to process what was going on while standing still and frozen. How did he discover him? And why is she now with him? Marie was his love and everything... "Don't worry," she said. I am not intending to harm you. I simply desired to see you and the man you have become.

He stood there motionless with his gun still in his hand because he didn't know what to say.

She said as she started to leave, "I must go now." However, do not worry; we will meet again."

He sat back and watched as she vanished into the shadows, leaving him to try to understand what had just transpired. Because he was aware that this was only the beginning of an extremely risky and potentially fatal mission, he was on high alert.

CHAPTER VI

The Pain of the Past

Sarah's eyes widened in amazement. James, the man we had been looking for for a long time, was standing in front of her and appeared to be just as dashing and dangerous as ever.

"Why did you release him?" Aron's response to Sarah's question about Silence was, "But as I looked into his eyes, he saw something she never expected to see: pain."

At the Agnès, Sarah was Aron's introduction. "What are you doing here, James?" In an effort to maintain her tone, Marie asked.

His smirk had been replaced by a sad smile as he replied, "I could ask you the same thing." However, I suppose that isn't what matters right now.

When James asked Marie to sit down with him on a nearby bench, Marie was surprised. He had always been a mystery to her, and she had no idea he would open up to her in this way.

He said, staring off into the distance, "I've been thinking a lot lately about my past—about how I got here and where I came from."

As James started to tell his story, Marie listened intently. He talked about his early years, when he lived in poverty and never knew his father. He described how he was left to fend for himself on the streets after his mother passed away. He expressed his despair and rage at the world for never giving him a chance.

When he turned to face Marie, he said, "I know what I've done is wrong." I am aware that I have caused a great deal of suffering. However, all I wanted to do was make a difference and demonstrate to the world that I was more than just a homeless person with nothing to offer.

Marie wanted to help James, but she couldn't let that affect her judgment. She had a job to do, and he remained a dangerous criminal. She couldn't help but wonder, however, as she looked at him, if there was more to his story and if there might be a way to assist him in finding redemption.

James noticed what she was thinking and said, "I'm not asking for your forgiveness." However, I merely wanted you to be aware of my rationale. Moreover, you should also do what your heart tells you to do. You know what I mean. After that, he got up, gave Marie a small nod, and then left, leaving her to consider the complicated and difficult past of the man she had been looking for so long.

Marie sat on the bench for a long time after James had left, lost in thought.Although she had always known that he was more than just a villain, she had no idea how much he had to suffer.

She couldn't shake the feeling that she had just been a part of something much bigger and more complicated than she had ever imagined as she finally got up and went back to her apartment. She couldn't help but wonder if he could get out of this mud and help him recover from his past wounds.

She discovered that James had had a troubled childhood marked by neglect and abuse as she dove deeper into his past. James's father was an emotionally and physically abusive man who came from a poor family. When he was young, his mother died, and he had no one to turn to for comfort or support.

James grew up with a deep resentment towards society and those who had privileged upbringings. He believed that the world had wronged him and that retaliation was the only way to even the scales. As a result, he became a criminal mastermind who sought to wreak havoc on those who had everything he had never had, leading him down a path of fraud and crime.

Marie, on the other hand, discovered as she dug deeper that James felt more than resentment and rage.He showed compassion and kindness at times, helping the less fortunate and giving them a chance at a better life. It appeared as though James had two sides—the villain and the hero—that were constantly at odds with one another.

Marie was determined to help James find peace and put an end to his destructive ways, despite the fact that she knew it would be difficult.She watched his every move for months, putting the events of his past together and looking for a way to find the good in him.

She finally stumbled upon an opportunity one day. James was being held in a prison with a high level of security after being taken in by the authorities. Marie planned to finish what she started because it was the only way to end his pain. Pain is always tied to the past, and the past can never be erased; it hurts over and over again. She, like Marie, remembered Aron, realising that she, too, was doing wrong and betraying Aron, to whom she meant a lot.She made her way to the prison and visited Aron in his cell with a heavy heart. They talked about his past and the reasons he did what he did for hours. In addition, as she spoke with him, she observed his expression shift from one of rage and pain to one of understanding and tranquility.

In that instant, Marie realised that her mission was not just about stopping a villain; rather, it was about saving a soul. She was the one in charge of making Aron's arrest, against the assertion that he could be trying to betray the country for his love. That day, she left the prison with a renewed sense of purpose and the determination to continue her work and assist everyone in obtaining the vengeance he so desperately desired. Sarah's eyes widened in amazement. James, the man we had been looking for for a long time, was standing in front of her and appeared to be just as dashing and dangerous as ever.

"Why did you release him?" Aron's response to Sarah's question about Silence was, "But as I looked into his eyes, he saw something she never expected to see: pain."

At the Agnès, Sarah was Aron's introduction. "What are you doing here, James?" In an effort to maintain her tone, Marie asked.

His smirk had been replaced by a sad smile as he replied, "I could ask you the same thing." However, I suppose that isn't what matters right now.

When James asked Marie to sit down with him on a nearby bench, Marie was surprised. He had always been a mystery to her, and she had no idea he would open up to her in this way.

He said, staring off into the distance, "I've been thinking a lot lately about my past—about how I got here and where I came from."

As James started to tell his story, Marie listened intently. He talked about his early years, when he lived in poverty and never knew his father. He described how he was left to fend for himself on the streets after his mother passed away. He expressed his despair and rage at the world for never giving him a chance.

When he turned to face Marie, he said, "I know what I've done is wrong." I am aware that I have caused a great deal of suffering. However, all I wanted to do was make a difference and demonstrate to the world that I was more than just a homeless person with nothing to offer.

Marie felt an ache of compassion towards James, but she was unable to let that cloud her judgment. She had a job to do, and he remained a dangerous criminal. She couldn't help but wonder, however, as she looked at him, if there was more to his story and if there might be a way to assist him in finding redemption.

James noticed what she was thinking and said, "I'm not asking for your forgiveness." However, I merely wanted you to be aware of my rationale. Moreover, you should also do what your heart tells you to do. You know what I mean. After that, he got up, gave Marie a small nod, and then left, leaving her to consider the complicated and difficult past of the man she had been looking for so long.

Marie sat on the bench for a long time after James had left, lost in thought.Although she had always known that he was more than just a villain, she had no idea how much he had to suffer.

She couldn't shake the feeling that she had just been a part of something much bigger and more complicated than she had ever imagined as she finally got up and went back to her apartment. She couldn't help but wonder if he could get out of this mud and help him recover from his past wounds.

She discovered that James had had a troubled childhood marked by neglect and abuse as she dove deeper into his past. James's father was an emotionally and physically abusive man who came from a poor family. When he was young, his mother died, and he had no one to turn to for comfort or support.

James grew up with a deep resentment towards society and those who had privileged upbringings. He believed that the world had wronged him and that retaliation was the only way to even the scales. As a result, he became a criminal mastermind who sought to wreak havoc on those who had everything he had never had, leading him down a path of fraud and crime.

Marie, on the other hand, discovered as she dug deeper that James felt more than resentment and rage.He showed compassion and kindness at times, helping the less fortunate and giving them a chance at a better life. It appeared as though James had two sides—the villain and the hero—that were constantly at odds with one another.

Marie was determined to help James find peace and put an end to his destructive ways, despite the fact that she knew it would be difficult.She watched his every move for months, putting the events of his past together and looking for a way to find the good in him.

She finally stumbled upon an opportunity one day. James was being held in a prison with a high level of security after being taken in by the authorities. Marie planned to finish what she started because it was the only way to end his pain. Pain is always tied to the past, and the past can never be erased; it hurts over and over again. She, like Marie, remembered Aron, realising that she, too, was doing wrong and betraying Aron, to whom she meant a lot.She made her way to the prison and visited Aron in his cell with a heavy heart. They talked about his past and the reasons he did what he did for hours. In addition, as she spoke with him, she observed his expression shift from one of rage and pain to one of understanding and tranquility.

In that instant, Marie realised that her mission was not just about stopping a villain; rather, it was about saving a soul. She was the one in charge of making Aron's arrest, against the assertion that he could be trying to betray the country for his love. That day, she left the prison with a renewed sense of purpose and the determination to continue her work and assist everyone in obtaining the vengeance he so desperately desired.

CHAPTER VII

The Tipping Point

Marie and Aaron had put in a lot of effort to find out what was behind James's plan. They were determined to put an end to his evil plans once and for all because they were aware that they posed a threat not only to their nation but to the entire world.

For a number of months, the two spies had been following clues and deciphering obscure messages, each new piece of information bringing them closer to the truth. They finally made a breakthrough.They found poems and notes detailing James' evil plan in a secret journal that belonged to him.

Putting together the clues and deciphering the poems, Marie and Aaron spent hours studying the journal. They quickly came to the conclusion that the poems contained more than just cryptic messages; they served as a road map to James's ultimate objective, which was to launch a nuclear missile in the name of another nation, triggering a nuclear war between them. Marie was aware of James' hatred of people, so she made the decision to grab Aron's hand and do the right thing no matter what. However, as she got closer to her goal, she noticed that James was becoming uneasy. She couldn't shake the feeling that James made her work for him by manipulating her emotions, but he eventually found out who she really was.

She heard a soft knock at the door one night while reviewing her notes in her hotel room. She froze, and her thoughts raced. Did this mark the end? Was she finally caught by James?

She summoned her courage and walked towards the door with her hand on the handle. She then opened it with a deep breath.

A hooded figure whose face was obscured stood on the opposite side, shrouded in shadow. There was only silence for a brief period of time—a tense, oppressive silence that made it seem as though it was getting closer to her.

The figure then spoke with a voice as icy as ice.

He said, "It's over, Marie." We've had a hard time with you for far too long. You'll have to pay the price now."

When Marie realised that her cover had been compromised, her heart broke. She tried to sneak a peek after gathering the scattered courage.

The figure took a step forward and held a gun. As she tried to think of a way out, Marie's mind raced. She then hurled the lamp from the bedside table at her attacker with a sudden spurt of inspiration.

As the lamp smashed into his head, the figure stumbled back, giving Marie just enough time to grab her own weapon and fire. She let out a sigh of relief as the body fell to the ground.

"Why the hell did you do that, you know how scared I was..." Aron said.

"I have never frightened...." "Yeah, you did, or let's keep it a secret between us. " "I'm not sure what you're talking about," she smirked, "but just like Lotus, you were in mud but never let a drop of water touch you. Hats off...""Thanks, but it wasn't me." "Yeah, I know," I say, trying to sound intelligent.

"None of this... did I do something wrong?" "Whatever, but I have to say you haven't changed as much as you used to," "and now that you're with me, I have no reason to fear... "The two of them stood in silence for a moment, evaluating one another. "You kept thinking of yourself..."James was a tall man with blue eyes that pierced the air. His muscular build indicated how many hours he had spent perfecting his skills. He was a formidable foe, and the fact that he had eluded capture for such a considerable amount of time was evidence of his cunning and intelligence.

Marie hears James saying, "I have evidence that links you to the crimes you've committed." Additionally, he would have a team of agents who are already closing our location. As she spoke, Aron's smirk dissipated, and she had the fleeting impression that he had an expression of fear in his eyes. But then it went away, and he regained his confidence.

He stated, "You won't get away with this." "You are a hacker; use your superpower; and about the agents, I am waiting for them on the ground." As she watched him being led away, she couldn't help but think of all the lives he had destroyed and the people he had hurt. She was pleased that she had brought him to justice, as he was now going to pay for his crimes.

She hacked into the setup at James, who was a good professional because he had evidence that she was the perpetrator.

"I'm just messed up," she told herself.There was no way out because Aron was wanted by the government, and Marie and James were also. "Hey, let's make a deal," she said to James. "Deal, oh, I like it. What is it?""We would give you the key to the satellite to activate the missile," she explained, "and why would you do that, and if I can, I can easily have them.""No, you can't because the system requires the president's retina test, and in exchange, I want you to give your name for blast," she explained."No, I will not, but what is your profit in that?" "Don't try to trick me...

what about Aron?"

"Aron, I will kill him; he is still behind me this time." "Do you trust me?" "You must do so, or we will arrest you today or tomorrow, and if I am arrested, I will have no regrets after killing you.""Great ideas; okay, tomorrow at..."The day of the battle arrived, and Marie prepared for the fight of their lives. She was ready to confront James and his army of rogue agents, dressed in their finest black suits and armed with their gadgets and weapons.

They could feel the tension rising as they got closer to James's hideout. As they moved through the shadows, their steps made an echo in the still night. They were a formidable duo of spies with the goal of saving the world.

An army of heavily armed men greeted them when they finally reached James's hideout. However, they accommodated her and let her go quietly.

"None of your business," "those dogs are too good, where do you get them?" "Do you have the codes?"

"Here," she said, handing him the suitcase, which he opened and checked.

"You know you were my best man, but now that you've betrayed me, there's no way I can trust you again." "Really?"

"yeah," "I believe you informed me that your friend would be arriving soon.""Who friends?" "I don't have any," I say, "and I'm sure you wouldn't be happy to see them..."The mission was not going according to plan, and Maria found herself in a dangerous situation. "I think you have let me know as your friend will be arriving soon." She had been taken captive by James and imprisoned in a cell deep within his covert base. She was aware that she had to get away before he could get any information from her.

Maria was determined to escape because she was not one to give up easily. She carefully surveyed her surroundings and noticed that the door did not have windows and was made of solid steel. There was only one entry and exit, and two heavily armed guards stood guard over it.

In an effort to find a way out, she sat down on the bed and closed her eyes. She suddenly recalled a secret device she had concealed in her shoe. She quickly got it back and used it to break the door lock.

Maria was able to evade the guards and reach the surface after they were taken by surprise. She was aware that she needed to get as far away from the base as possible.

There was a rumbling all around the gangster and terrorist groups as James's friends arrived, and they were told that any secret codes that cost billions of dollars in the market were there.

CHAPTER VIII

The Final Showdown

As Marie made her way to the meeting place, the sun was just beginning to rise. She was determined despite her nervousness. She had come too far, and at this point, she was not going to relent.

She knew that she had to stop James because she had finally discovered the truth about him and his motives. James was a brilliant individual who had been driven to madness by his past experiences of pain and suffering. His so-called friends had to stop him because he had vented his rage and frustration to the world.

With the assistance of the government's army and all remaining individuals, they captured him.

At the jail, she said, "Good morning, James."

He replied with a calm and steady "Good morning." I've been anticipating your arrival.

She said, "I know." "And I'm here to thwart your scheme."

James said with a hint of rage in his voice, "You can't stop me." "I have come too far for someone like you to stop me."

Marie said, "I'm not just anyone." As a spy, I will not permit you to kill innocent people.

James chuckled. Do you believe you can stop me?You're just a stupid girl who got herself into a situation she couldn't handle.

Marie tightened her grip on her gun. She stated, "I'm not just a foolish girl." I am a woman who has faced and conquered her fears. James, I will stop you.

Their tension was palpable as they stood there for a short while. Then, without prior notice,

"What say?" "We should not keep him alive." Aron said, "probably," and they gave James a gun. Marie felt a sharp pain in her side as the shots rang out across the empty field. However, she did not let it deter her. Determined to put an end to James for good, she fired incessantly.

James lay motionless and lifeless on the ground.

She simply expressed gratitude for being alive and contributing to the fight against evil. She stepped into the dimly lit room and instinctively reached for the gun at her waist, having overcome her fears. She would always be a spy, prepared for anything the world could throw at her. She had learned from her training to be cautious and to never let her guard down, even in the simplest of situations.

On the other side, Aron's bloodied body showed that he had been shot before killing Marie; he jumped and accepted it happily.

Because she was a spy, she would always be prepared for whatever the outside world might throw at her. She was on a mission to bring about peace and justice for the wronged.

He advised her to "run, Marie," and that "this government will find you guilty even if you provide proof." Run... Despite the fact that she was getting ready for what might transpire next, she was still unable to avoid feeling a slight sense of sadness. She had witnessed a great deal of violence and suffering in her line of work, including the loss or destruction of numerous lives.

She then, however, recalled the reasons she had chosen this path. She recalled the agony and suffering she had experienced as well as the ways in which the evil forces had torn apart her friends and family.

In addition, she was aware that she was having an impact and that she was contributing to the end of the world's hatred and violence.

She took a deep breath and moved forward, ready for whatever came next, as she heard footsteps getting closer. Because she was a spy, she would always be up to the challenges of her mission, which was to bring peace and justice to a world that so badly needed them.

CHAPTER IX

Whatever....

She had always known that her life as a spy would be full of danger and excitement, but she had no idea that it would eventually lead her to this point. the man she had been chasing for so long.He was the bad guy who was responsible for a series of terrorist attacks that killed a lot of innocent people. And then it stopped. She tried to calm down by taking a deep breath. It was this—the final battle. She was well prepared and well trained, but she knew James was no joke. She couldn't let her guard down for a second because he was a clever and dangerous opponent.

"I'm glad we finally get to meet face to face," James said, his eyes closed as he grabbed a small note book from James' coat and fled.

She responded in a calm and steady voice, "The feeling is not mutual."

"Ah, but you must admit that this is what you've worked for all these years, isn't it?" James mocked. the opportunity to humiliate me and bring about justice for all those I've wronged."

She stated firmly, "Justice is precisely what I plan to bring."

"Is it truly that easy?" James inquired with a sneering smile. Do you really believe that stopping me will solve all of the problems in the world? that you'll make everyone happy and peaceful?"

She responded, "I know that it won't solve all the problems in the world, but it's a start." I must also try. To make a difference in the world, I must do something.

Anything.

"And my situation?" James asked, moving closer to her. What about my difficulties and suffering? What are the reasons behind my actions?

She didn't back down, "I understand that you've been through a lot," she said. However, this does not excuse your actions, which have resulted in the loss of life and damage. "Your crimes have to be paid for."

"And you think that if you stop me, it will bring closure to everyone who was hurt by what I did?" James asked, raising his voice. "You think that if you stop me, it will bring peace to everyone who has been hurt?"

She said, her resolve growing stronger, "It won't bring back the lives lost, but it will give the families of the victims a sense of justice."

"And how about your own tranquility?" James asked, his eyes getting smaller. How about your own suffering? "What about the events in your life that you've been through?"

She said, "That's not relevant," refusing to be swayed. "I must do the right thing, no matter what."

"And what if what you think is right isn't what it actually is?" James inquired, speaking in a whisper. "What if the right thing is something that you can't even imagine?"

She said, her voice firm, "I don't care." I must attempt "I must act in a moral manner."

She couldn't help but reflect on all of the difficulties she had encountered up to this point as she moved through the city. Every time she had to deal with danger, she always prevailed. She had confronted and overcome her fears. Additionally, she was now facing her greatest obstacle to date: James, the villain's name.

Her anticipation ran high as she made her way to James' headquarters. She was prepared for anything, having planned this mission for weeks. She was prepared to confront James and bring him to justice.

She saw James's picture as she approached the building; his eyes were fixed on her. With her head held high, she confidently approached him.

She spoke in a steady voice, "James," "I'm here to get justice for you."

James chuckled. He said, "You're just a silly little girl." "Do you believe you can bring me down?"

She grinned. She stated, "I don't think so. I know."

She immediately got to work, preparing to confront James and bring him to justice. Because she was a spy, she would always be prepared for whatever the outside world might throw at her.

Because there was still something up, she was aware that James would not end his life in that manner.

CHAPTER X

The Final Confrontation

She switched to Lily to retrieve the item that Mugged had taken.

Lily took a deep breath and prepared herself for the final confrontation as she approached the notorious James Blackwood's hideout and changed into Lily to retrieve the stolen item. She had been following James for several months, gathering information and devising a strategy to eliminate him permanently. She was a spy who was determined to bring about reconciliation and justice for the wronged.

Lily experienced a surge of adrenaline as she entered the building. She moved quickly and silently, taking out each of James's operatives one by one despite being surrounded by them. She was skilled in espionage and did not hesitate to use her abilities to defeat her adversary.

In the end, she made it to the room where James was waiting.As if he had been anticipating her all along, he smiled as he sat at his desk. He said, "Welcome, Lily," his voice full of sarcasm. I've been anticipating your arrival.

Lily did not answer. As she prepared for the final battle, she simply stood there with her eyes fixed on James's. Their eyes were locked in a silent struggle of wills as they stood there for what seemed like an eternity.

At long last, James ended the quietness. "Don't you know why you're here?" "His voice was low and menacing," he said. I need you to stop me. to prevent me from acquiring what is rightfully mine and taking what I want."

Lily's response was firm and steady: "I'm here to bring you to justice."

James chuckled. Justice? "What knowledge do you have of justice?" He grinned. You believe that you are so good and pure. However, you have no idea what I've been through or endured. To safeguard what is mine, I'm doing what needs to be done to survive.

Lily did not hesitate. She was aware that James was dangerous and that he would do anything to achieve his goals. But no matter what, she was determined to stop him. James arose from his seat with a knife in his hand as she moved forward.

He growled, "Lily, you should have stayed out of this. You are completely ignorant of the situation."

Lily did not answer. She proceeded to raise her own weapon and prepare for the last confrontation.

Their weapons rang out in the quiet room as they clashed in a steel flurry. Lily moved faster than James. She was an expert in her field, and she used her knowledge to outwit James at every opportunity.

Lily struck the final blow at the end. In defeat, James collapsed to the ground. When Lily realised that it was finally over, she stood over him, gasping for air.

She stopped one of the most dangerous villains of her time and was a spy. In addition, as she considered the events of the previous few months, she became aware that she had discovered something that was significantly more valuable than the fulfilment of a successful mission: a reason to keep fighting for what was right and a sense of purpose.

CHAPTER XI

The End of an Era

She watched as James was taken away in handcuffs as she stood there. She couldn't help but feel a twinge of sadness in her heart in spite of everything he had done. She couldn't help but wonder if there was a different outcome that could have been achieved now that she had come to understand the pain that had led him down the path of evil.

She was overcome with emotion as she left the scene. She felt a variety of emotions: relief that justice had finally been done, but also a profound sense of loss for everything that had gone wrong.

She felt a sense of calm, though, as she wiped away her tears and gazed up at the brilliant blue sky. She had successfully completed her task, and she had done so with honour and integrity. She had overcome her fears and prevailed.

She couldn't help but feel proud of everything she had accomplished as she thought back on all the difficulties she had overcome. She was a spy, and she would remain one for the rest of her life, prepared for anything the outside world might throw at her.

She had a good reason to keep fighting for what was right, and she would do so with all of her strength. She would always be there, ready to defend the innocent and bring peace and justice to those who had been wronged, whenever there was injustice in the world.

She walked off into the sunset with a grin on her face, prepared for whatever the future might bring. She also knew, as she vanished from view, that she had found her true calling and would always be remembered as one of the greatest spies ever.

Aron was by her side, shoulder to shoulder breathing. "HOW did you know it wasn't over?" Aron asked. "I have worked with him for many years, and I had a feeling that he could not stop there." She responded, "What else was there in the book?" He asked, "You can do that stuff alone, but you intently gave him a gun and got him to shoot and send me... She questioned, and he smiled, "It was all you..." There is a blood channel that runs through me.

CHAPTER XII

The Secret Mission

She was on a mission to thwart James's evil plans—the infamous criminal who had wreaked such havoc on the world. However, she received a message from her superiors as she moved deeper into enemy territory. They had a secret mission for her that was just as important, if not more so, than the one she was currently working on.

She was tasked with finding a confidential piece of information that had been misplaced. It was information that, if released to the public, could devastate the entire world. Since no one else could carry out the task, her superiors had assigned it to her.

She accepted the assignment with courage and determination, as she always did. She was conscious of both the necessity and the danger of the task at hand. She was the only one who could save the world from certain doom.

Using all of her training and abilities, she made her way to the location where the information was stored to avoid detection. She had to overcome many challenges along the way, but her bravery and intelligence enabled her to do so.

Her greatest obstacle to date awaited her when she finally got there. A group of highly skilled soldiers guarded the information and refused to give it up easily. However, she refused to back down because she was prepared for anything.

She engaged in a fierce battle and managed to defeat the guards and retrieve the information by employing both her combat skills and her wit. She won the battle and got the information safely out of the encounter.

Marie was no stranger to perilous missions because she was a highly skilled spy. However, she had never been assigned anything quite like this before. She was tasked with breaking into a secret facility deep inside enemy territory to gather vital information that could change the war's course.

Marie was aware of the substantial risks and high stakes. But she wouldn't back down from a challenge because she was a true hero to her country and the world. Because she had received training in the art of espionage, she was well prepared to deal with anything that awaited her.

She worked on her cover story, studied maps of the enemy territory, and prepared for the mission for weeks. She was supposed to pretend to be a scientist so she could enter the facility and blend in with the other workers. She worked on her fake accent and memorised the specifics of her fake identity until she was sure she could fool people.

She finally had the day to set out on the mission. A group of special forces soldiers dropped Marie into hostile territory with the intention of waiting for her when she returned with the information she had been assigned.

Marie persevered despite the long and perilous journey, motivated by her sense of duty and love for her nation. She eventually got to the facility and managed to blend in with the other workers. Over time, she gained their trust and the access she needed to finish her mission.

Pretending to be a typical scientist, she diligently documented everything she saw and photographed over the course of several weeks. Because she was aware that even the tiniest error could cost her not only the mission but also her life, she was always vigilant.

Marie finally had all the information she needed after what seemed like an eternity. She returned to the extraction point, where the soldiers from the special forces were waiting for her. She was finally free to exhale a sigh of relief after they brought her out of hostile territory.

Upon her return, she was hailed as a hero, and the information she had gathered was crucial to the enemy's defeat. She was a true hero in the eyes of her nation and the world because she successfully completed a risky mission.

CHAPTER XIII

The Weapon Fails

The mission was intended to be routine. merely obtaining a top-secret weapon from a distant facility deep within hostile territory. But things started going wrong as soon as she got off the helicopter. The unanticipated resistance from the hostile soldiers guarding the facility came first. Then, a rival spy agency suddenly showed up, determined to get the weapon for themselves. She then heard a strange hissing sound coming from the package she was carrying, just as she thought she had finally secured the weapon and was making her way out.

After a brief pause, she realised what she needed to do. She hurled the weapon as far away from herself as she could with a strength born of desperate need. She felt the shockwave rip through her just as she hit the ground and covered her head with her arms. She heard a huge explosion.

She was lying in a shallow crater surrounded by charred ruins when she opened her eyes. She looked around as she struggled to get to her feet, confused and lost. The weapon was ineffective. Everything had vanished as a result of some catastrophic malfunction. The facility, the soldiers of the enemy, and the rival spies In the span of a few seconds, it was all gone.

She was the only person to survive. She also realised with a growing sense of despair that she was also the only person who knew the truth about what had just occurred as she stumbled through the charred remains looking for any signs of life. She was the only person who was aware of the weapon's capabilities.

She had to leave that place. She had to return to her superiors to issue a warning. She was obligated to ensure that this did not occur again. She began to run and made her way through the debris until she came across an operational vehicle. She drove away from the scene as quickly as she could after hotwiring the engine.

When she finally made it back to headquarters, she was aware that she was in for a lengthy and difficult debriefing. However, she was up for anything. Because she was a spy, she would always be prepared for whatever the outside world might throw at her. She emerged stronger and more determined than ever after surviving the failure of a weapon that had the potential to destroy the world. She was regarded as a true hero by both her nation and the rest of the world, and she would always be prepared to meet any obstacle.

She was trained as a spy to deal with any circumstance. But she couldn't help but feel a little bit of fear as she stood there and stared at the broken weapon in front of her. The objective was to locate a potent weapon that would aid in world peace, but now it appeared as though their efforts had been in vain.

She was aware that she had to keep moving forward despite the setback. She was unable to let a minor setback prevent her from completing her mission. She rallied her team and began working on a new strategy with determination.

Soon enough, they found a clue that took them to a secret facility where the weapon was kept. She was able to sneak her team in unnoticed, despite the fact that it was heavily guarded.

They finally got to the weapon, which they were able to successfully retrieve.

Their mission, however, was far from over. They still needed to return the weapon to their superiors and ensure that it was used for good rather than evil. She was prepared for anything that might come her way, despite the long and perilous journey.

CHAPTER XIV

The Old Villain's Legacy

Aron had thought that James' death would put an end to their problems, but it turned out that he had left behind a legacy that could bring the world to its knees.The spy organization's agents discovered his final plan, a sinister scheme that, if left unchecked, would have devastating repercussions.

As they worked to unravel the plot and avert the disaster, he and her team were in a race against time. From the bustling cities of Europe to the remote deserts of the Middle East, they followed a clue trail. They faced challenges and obstacles that put their abilities and resolve to the test at every step.

Yet he was prepared. He had made too many sacrifices and travelled too far to give up now. He charged into battle, eliminating the adversaries one at a time until the facility was secured, guided by her team's support and her training and experience.

He paused for a moment to take her breath and reflect on everything he had accomplished since the mission.He had stopped a dangerous villain's final plan—a disaster that could have killed a lot of people—and made her a true hero in her country's eyes and the world's.

But even as he celebrated her victory, he was aware that there would always be new difficulties, conflicts, and threats to overcome.

He was determined to thwart the villain's remaining plans and ensure that no one else would suffer in the same way. He was prepared to confront the complex network of agents that the old villain had left behind. He had the knowledge and experience to locate them and eliminate them one by one.

He began by gathering information and putting together what little he knew about the remaining agents. He discovered that they were tasked with carrying out a series of perilous missions, each of which was meant to set the stage for the villain's ultimate goal of destabilising the world.

determined to stop them before they could carry out their plan, he died quickly. He carried out his work in complete secrecy, sneaking into and out of various nations and obtaining information wherever he could. He was not going to be discouraged, despite the challenging and risky nature of the job.

He discovered that the actual threat was much greater than he had anticipated as he dug deeper into the network's remnants. The villain had collaborated with a powerful and influential organization that possessed the manpower and resources necessary to carry out his plan globally.

He was aware that he needed to act quickly to put an end to the group before it was too late. He spent months compiling data and devising a strategy, collaborating with her agents to devise a plan that would enable them to eliminate the organisation and put an end to the villain's scheme for good.

The day finally arrived. He and her team advanced and quickly struck. They were able to bring down the organization's leaders and disrupt its operations because they were caught off guard. The evildoer's scheme was foiled immediately, and the world was safe once more.

He was overcome with pride and satisfaction as he thought back on the mission. He had overcome her greatest obstacle and won, proving once and for all that he was a hero. He also knew that he would always be prepared for anything the world could throw at her, no matter what the future held.

CHAPTER XV

The Return of Evil

Marie knew there was a problem as soon as she got the call. She had learned to trust her instincts as a spy, and at this very moment, they were telling her that she was needed back in the field. She had been working on a new project that would give her the opportunity to assist others in a way that was completely different from the spy work she usually did. However, she was being dragged back into the espionage industry at this point.

As Marie packed her belongings and got ready to leave, she felt a knot in her stomach. She had put in so much effort to forget the past and the dangers and pain that came with being a spy. However, she was now being summoned back into that world to confront the evil she believed she had defeated.

She was aware that she would not be travelling on her own. She gave her life to her fellow spies, who were among the best in the world. She could not help but feel a sense of unease as she got on the plane and headed back to the intelligence agency's headquarters.

The meeting was short and focused. A group of rogue agents had recently revolted, and they were attempting to acquire some of the world's most lethal weapons. Marie and her team were being summoned to put an end to their evil plans once and for all by stopping them.

Marie wanted to be successful. She was regarded as a true hero by both her nation and the rest of the world, and she refused to let anyone stand in her way. She couldn't help but feel excited as she gathered her team and began to plan their next move. She was eager to demonstrate her capabilities to the world because it had been a long time since she had worked in the field.

Marie, on the other hand, became aware as she began her mission that the reemergence of evil would not be simple. The rogue agents were well prepared and organized, and they were not afraid to go to any lengths to achieve their goals. If Marie and her team wanted to win the fight of their lives and save the world from the threat posed by their weapons, they would need to use every skill and trick in their arsenal.

Marie was not put off. Because she was a spy, she would always be prepared for whatever the outside world might throw at her. She set out, supported by her team, to halt the return of evil, put an end to the schemes of the rogue agents, and ensure the world's safety for good.

Looking out over the vast, churning ocean, she stood at the cliff's edge. Marie was aware, though, that perilous forces were operating beneath the tranquil surface of the sea. Because she was a spy, she would always be prepared for whatever the outside world might throw at her. However, the threat this time was different. The shady agents were back, and they were even more determined than ever to carry out the evil plans they had come up with.

Marie exhaled deeply to regain her strength. She needed to keep an eye out for her enemies and stay one step ahead of them. To fight for what was right and ensure the world's safety once and for all, she needed to be prepared for anything. She was determined to stop the shady agents' plans and bring about peace and justice for the wronged.

Marie was aware that the task in front of her was not going to be simple as she turned and began walking back to her base of operations. The rogue agents were clever and inventive, and they would stop at nothing to accomplish their objectives. But Marie didn't worry.

As Marie prepared for the upcoming mission, the following days were filled with intense training and preparation. She put in a lot of effort, learning new skills and studying the intelligence reports about the bad guys. She was determined to anticipate her adversaries' every move, stay one step ahead of them, and stop them before they could do any more harm.

Marie was prepared when the day finally arrived. She set out on her mission with both excitement and nerves in her heart. She made her way through the shadows quickly and quietly, avoiding detection. Naturally, the rogue agents were expecting her, but they were unprepared for Marie's skill and determination in the fight.

Marie played a dangerous game of cat and mouse with the rogue agents for hours, avoiding bullets and outwitting her foes at every opportunity. Marie was aware of the high stakes and the fact that one bad decision could mean the difference between life and death. However, she was an experienced veteran who maintained her composure and always considered her opponents in advance.

CHAPTER XVI

The New Threat

The most recent developments in her mission consumed Marie's thoughts as she made her way through the city's bustling streets. She was tasked with preventing the return of an evil that had been thought defeated for a long time.However, brand-new information suggested that the rogue agents were still present and posed a significant threat to the world.

Marie was determined to thwart their schemes and ensure the world's safety for good. However, she was aware that the path ahead would be difficult. The rogue agents were not afraid to use the powerful weapons they had at their disposal.

Marie received a message from her superiors as she walked. She was terrified despite the straightforward message. It stated, "The new threat has emerged." When Marie read the words, her heart broke. She was aware that this marked the beginning of a brand new and perilous period in her career as a spy.

Marie went to a secret location and met with her superiors there. They informed her of the new threat's specifics and the actions she needed to take to stop it. A potent weapon that had been acquired by the rogue agents had the potential to destroy the world. Marie was responsible for finding it and preventing the agents from using it.

In order to assist Marie in her mission, she was given a team of agents. Even though they all had a lot of experience and were well trained, Marie was aware that they would be up against a formidable foe. The shady agents were well-known for their deceit and skill at staying one step ahead of their adversaries.

In order to put an end to the rogue agents and save the world, Marie and her crew set out on their mission. They went to different places to find leads and gather information. They finally located the weapon's location.

Marie and her team got ready for the last confrontation. They were prepared for anything that might occur to them because they were aware that the rogue agents would not surrender without a fight. Although the battle was intense and lasted for hours, Marie and her team prevailed in the end. They had discovered the weapon and destroyed it, ending the shady agents' plans for good.

Marie quickly realised that she was up against a more formidable foe than she had anticipated as she continued to investigate the rogue agents. The shady agents were well-known for their deceit and ability to stay one step ahead of their foes, constantly coming up with novel ways to avoid capture.

Marie's task was to discover the truth about the latest scheme of the shady agents and put an end to their plans before they could do any more damage. A poetry book that she found among their belongings was the only lead she had. Marie was determined to decipher the book's cryptic messages, which pointed to a larger conspiracy.

She read the book page by page, carefully reading each line for any clues that might help her figure out the truth. She finally saw it at that point. The lines were from a poem that talked about a powerful weapon that was hidden deep in the jungle.

When Marie realised that this might be the break she needed to end the rogue agents once and for all, she felt a rush of excitement. She quickly gathered her supplies and set out into the jungle, her adrenaline pumping as she got closer to her objective.

Marie persevered despite the exhausting and lengthy journey because she was aware that the world was counting on her. She finally emerged from the foliage and saw the weapon after spending days traversing the dangerously dense jungle.

She had never seen anything like it before. It was a machine with a seemingly endless array of gears and wires and an energy that was both terrifying and amazing. As she looked for any indications of danger, Marie approached the weapon with care, and her senses were on high alert.

However, there was no threat. The weapon lay dormant, awaiting its moment of activation to unleash its destructive power on the world. Marie knew that she had to destroy the weapon to prevent it from falling into the wrong hands and causing untold destruction.

She dismantled the machine piece by piece, racing her mind and working quickly until nothing but a heap of scrap metal remained. Marie also realised that she had accomplished her goal, which gave her a sense of relief and pride. She had ended the plans of the rogue agents and ensured the world's safety for good.

CHAPTER XVII

A Trail of Clues

Marie found herself following a trail of clues that led her to an old, forgotten book of poems as she dove deeper into the investigation of the rogue agents. She knew that this book was the key to unlocking the secrets of the rogue agents because of the strange markings on the cover and the cryptic poems inside.

She carefully analysed the poems, looking for messages or hidden meanings in the language. Marie struggled to comprehend the poems' strange, cryptic language, but she was determined to decipher them. She was smarter than the rogue agents, but she knew that they were smart.

She looked through the book for hours, searching for any clues that might lead her to the hideout of the rogue agents. She was so focused on her work that she barely noticed time passing, and before she knew it, it was past midnight.

She finally discovered something just as she was about to give up. a hidden sequence of numbers and letters in one of the poems' words. She recognised this immediately as a code and the key to locating the rogue agents.

After quickly copying the code, Marie returned to her headquarters. She was eager to begin cracking the code and share her discovery with her team. She was prepared for anything the world could throw at her, even though she was aware that this was only the beginning of a long and dangerous journey.

Aron was accustomed to overcoming challenges as a spy, but the search for the truth was proving to be her greatest challenge to date. She had always been a persistent individual motivated by a sense of duty and a passion for justice. However, this mission was unique. She was fighting this time not only for her country but also for the entire world.

The rogue agents had discovered a book of mysterious poems that appeared to contain the key to their most recent evil scheme. Aron had to figure out the poem's meaning and decipher it before it was too late. She looked at the words and their hidden meanings for a long time, but she couldn't find the answers.

Aron received a crucial clue just as she believed she had reached a dead end. a note that one of the agents, who had been captured and was currently in custody, had left behind. "The truth is hidden in plain sight," read the note. "In the midst of the darkness, look for the light."

Aron was determined to uncover the truth, and she was aware that the only way to do so was to reach the light's source. She gathered her team and set out for the far-flung mountains, where it was said that the light shone brightest.

Aron persevered despite the long and treacherous journey. She was a true hero in every sense of the word and was determined to protect the world from evil agents.

They were greeted by a breathtaking view as they reached the mountain's summit. The sky was splattered with pink and orange hues as the sun set. A lighthouse that stood out against the pitch-black background was in the middle of it all.

Aron and her team arrived at the lighthouse, and what they found inside was shocking. They discovered that the light was more than just an illumination source; it was also a knowledge source. They also discovered the solution to the obscure poem that had eluded them for so long within its walls.

CHAPTER XVIII

A Journey to the Unknown

Aron was determined to bring the rogue agents to justice and solve the mystery of the poems. For weeks, he had been working on this case, poring over every sentence and verse for any clues that might lead him to their hideout. He was determined to get to the bottom of the poems, despite the fact that they were obscure and difficult to comprehend.

He encountered difficulties that put his resolve and strength to the test as he moved deeper into the unknown. But she didn't give up.

He took safety measures because he was aware that the rogue agents were dangerous. He equipped himself with the most recent weapons and technology and ensured that he was always aware of his surroundings. He was determined to complete his mission successfully, no matter what.

He felt like he was getting closer to the truth with each step he took. He deciphered the codes, followed the hints, and pieced together the poems' mystery. Finally, he found himself standing in front of the hideout of the rogue agents, prepared to confront them and thwart their evil schemes.

He pushed the door open and entered the room while his heart was pounding in his chest. He was prepared for anything that could come his way and determined to complete his mission successfully. He would not disappoint the world's hopes for her.

With hints from the poem book in his possession, Aronset embarks on a journey to discover the truth about the latest rogue agent scheme.In order to decipher the meanings contained in the obscure verses, he travelled to far-flung locations, traversing treacherous terrain and putting himself in harm's way.

Aron encountered increasing difficulties as he advanced in his investigation. He had to deal with armed guards, outwit sophisticated security systems, and even go undercover to get into important places. But despite everything, he remained steadfast in his mission, motivated by his desire to safeguard the world and innocent people.

Aron finally located the secret base of the rogue agents after searching for many weeks. It was a fortified fortress that was guarded by a group of highly skilled soldiers and kept safe by the most recent in cutting-edge technology. But that didn't stop Aron. He was prepared for this one as well because he had previously encountered similar obstacles.

Aron approached the base with a determined expression, ready to end the rogue agents' reign of terror once and for all. He was a true hero, motivated by his love of justice and unwavering dedication to improving the world. and he wouldn't back down until his job was done.

CHAPTER XIX

The Road to Redemption

For weeks, Aron had been following the shady agents' tracks, and he was getting closer to the truth every day. He had deciphered a number of the poems in the book and assembled bits of information that led him to believe that the shady agents had a big surprise in store. something that would alter their perception of the world.

Aron was determined to put an end to them and bring about world peace and justice once and for all. Since he first became a spy, he had come a long way and learned a lot about who he was and what he could do. He had overcome numerous obstacles, but each time he had emerged victorious.

However, this mission was different. This time, he was fighting not only for his country but also for himself. He had witnessed the suffering that the shady agents had inflicted, and he was not going to let it happen again. Although he was a spy, he was also a genuine human being.

Aron continued his journey by looking for information and following the hints. He travelled to far-flung, perilous locations and took risks he never anticipated. However, he did all of it for the greater good. He was more than just a spy; he was a true hero to his country and the world.

He took a deep breath and prepared for what lay ahead as he finally reached the location where he believed the rogue agents were hiding. He had encountered numerous dangers and obstacles, but he was prepared. Because he was a spy, he would always be prepared for whatever the outside world threw at him. He was determined to end the shady agents' plans once and for all and bring peace and justice to those who had been wronged.

Marie realised that he was getting closer and closer to the truth as he continued on his journey. He felt more and more determined to end the shady agents' plans once and for all with each step. He was aware that the world was relying on him, and he would not disappoint them.

He deciphered the poem book's clues as he travelled to various locations, revealing secrets and unravelling the mystery of the rogue agents' plans. He found out that their ultimate objective was to cause global disorder and destruction, and it was up to him to stop them.

He worked tirelessly to combine the clues and locate leads, as Marie was determined to solve the puzzle. Despite the risk and uncertainty of the journey, Marie remained steadfast in her mission.

He was forced to navigate his way through a web of deceit and manipulation as he dove deeper into the mystery and encountered unexpected turns. But he didn't back down. He was a spy, so he was accustomed to working under pressure.

Marie eventually discovered that he was at the centre of the plot and was able to confront the rogue agents. With the world's fate on the line, it was a dramatic and intense battle. Marie, on the other hand, maintained his composure and skill to outwit his adversaries.

However, this mission was unique. The shady agents were well-known for their deceit and skill at staying one step ahead of their adversaries. They had established a community of devoted followers, and their influence was widespread.

She was not, however, discouraged. She was certain that she would be able to overcome even more difficult obstacles in the future. She had the knowledge, experience, and drive to succeed.

She was aware that she possessed the key to victory as she deciphered the cryptic poems' hidden meanings. She was prepared for anything the world could throw at her, even though the road ahead would be long and dangerous.

She felt a growing sense of self-assurance and resolve as she moved forward. She was more than just a spy; she was a real hero to her nation and the world. She also knew that she would prevail and bring peace and justice to the wronged as she continued her journey into the unknown.

stopped for good, and it was her job to make sure their evil plans were foiled. She was determined to acquire the information she required, and the poems held the key to unraveling the mystery of their ultimate objective.

She went to far-flung places, braved perilous terrain, and faced numerous obstacles. She carried on with her mission despite the odds and never lost sight of her ultimate objective. She used her skills to stay one step ahead of the rogue agents, making use of her training as a spy.

She came across allies who were also fighting for the same cause as her. They worked together to decipher the poems and discover their hidden meanings. She was determined to complete the journey, which was fraught with danger and ambiguity.

They finally discovered the truth about the schemes of the rogue agents. She was aware that she needed to act quickly to stop the sinister plot, which posed a threat to society as a whole. She prepared for the last stand and gathered her allies.

CHAPTER XX

The Final Showdown

As the two adversaries faced off in the deserted warehouse, the tension was palpable. The world's fate was at stake in the final confrontation between the hero and the villain. The hero, who had endured so much hardship and faced so many difficulties, was determined to put an end to the evil plans of the villain for good.

On the other hand, the villain was just as determined to see his plans come to pass. The hero was aware of his strategies, but he had been playing a mind game with her to try to get her off track and confused. She held her ground and was prepared to face the evildoer head-on.

The villain abruptly showed them his final card as they stood there facing each other. "I have a secret weapon that will guarantee my victory, even though you have been a thorn in my side for a long time," he said with a smirk.

The news surprised the hero, but she didn't let it shake her. She was aware that this would be her last chance to stop the villain and that she needed to be at her best.

She said firmly, "I'm not afraid of your tricks." "I'm prepared for whatever the world throws at me."

"That's what you think," said the villain with a grin. "But you and everything you stand for will be destroyed by this weapon."

He then pointed a small, handheld weapon at the hero.It was a mind-control device that could control anyone it was pointed at, which she only learned about too late.

However, the hero was not easily controlled. She jumped into action right away, launching herself at the bad guy and wresting the device from his grasp. As they fought for the weapon, the two of them fell to the ground and exchanged blows.

The hero finally prevailed after a prolonged and intense struggle. She had successfully eliminated the villain and destroyed the mind-control device.

She couldn't help but feel relieved as she stood there, taking a breath and looking at the damage. It was done by her. She had brought about peace and justice for those who had been wronged, saving the world.

The hero then vanished into the shadows, preparing for whatever the world had in store for her next.

The stage was set for the ultimate battle between the hero and the villain as the sun rose over the horizon. It was time to put an end to this cat-and-mouse game that had been going on for far too long.

The heroine took in the scene before her from the cliff's edge. In order to be prepared for whatever the world might throw at her, she had spent her entire life preparing for this moment by honing her skills and perfecting her technique.

She also experienced a surge of self-assurance as she stood on the verge of victory. She was prepared for this battle, prepared to confront the villain and put an end to his terror for good.

She was confronted by a wall of darkness that surrounded the villain and appeared to be impenetrable as she stepped forward to engage him. The hero made a last-ditch effort to protect himself, but he didn't let that stop him. She could see through the illusions and solve the puzzles the villain had thrown at her. She was a master of the mind.

She then stepped forward and began the final game of cat and mouse with a determined expression in her eyes.

They fought back and forth, each trying to outthink the other with their intelligence and cunning.

It became abundantly clear as the battle progressed that the hero was gradually gaining the upper hand. She was able to stay one step ahead of the villain at every turn thanks to her training and experience.

Finally, the hero prevailed after what seemed like an eternity. The bad guy was defeated, his evil plans were thwarted, and the world was once again safe.

As she looked out over the landscape, the hero let out a triumphant laugh and felt a rush of excitement and joy. She had accomplished it, secured a brighter future for the world, and brought justice and peace to those who had been wronged.

She couldn't help but smile as she looked out over the horizon. She was confident that she was up to the challenge that lay ahead and was prepared for whatever the world might throw at her next.

CHAPTER XXI

The Poem Time

Years had passed since the defeat of the rogue agents, and the world had finally found peace and stability once again. The hero, now retired from her spy duties, had dedicated herself to helping others and making a positive impact on the world. But one day, she received a mysterious package in the mail. It contained a book of poems, written in code.

Intrigued, she took the book to a trusted friend, a codebreaker who had helped her on many of her missions in the past. Together, they worked to decipher the code, and what they found stunned them. The poems described the plans of a new group of rogue agents, who were plotting to cause chaos and destruction around the world.

The hero knew that she had to act quickly to stop this new threat. She gathered a team of former colleagues and set out on a journey to track down the rogue agents and put an end to their plans once and for all.

One of the poems in the book reads:

"Beneath the shadows of the night,
A plan is formed,
a dangerous sight.
A force of evil,
with power untold,
Will rise up and take control."

Another poem read:

"In the heart of the city,
where buildings touch the sky,
A secret hideout,
where they lie in wait,

With weapons at their side,
they'll make their play,
And unleash destruction on the world's fate."

The hero and her team worked tirelessly to decode the rest of the poems and find the location of the rogue agents' hideout. They were determined to bring peace and justice to those who had been wronged, just as they had always been. And with each step of their journey, they grew more confident in their ability to stop this new threat and keep the world safe once and for all.

"Beneath the moonlight's gentle glow A secret lies,
untold and slow The answers sought,
the truth to know A path to peace,
the way to go
The journey ahead,
fraught with strife Through trials and danger,
the risk of life The key to unlock,
the end in sight The truth to unfold,
in the darkest night
The shadows lurk,
with hidden intent The forces of evil,
a scourge well spent But fear not,
brave soul, for the battle's near And victory shall be yours,
with heart full of cheer
The quest to unravel,
the mystery untold The final showdown,
with tales untold The fight to end,
the victory to unfold A world at peace,
with justice bold."

It had been several years since the defeat of the rogue agents, and the world had finally found some semblance of peace. But for our hero, there was still work to be done. The poems that had been left behind by the agents were finally decoded, and they described their plans in detail.

The first poem read:

"Beneath the earth,
where roots entwine A weapon waits,
its power divine In secret kept,
beyond the light To unleash destruction,
in one fateful night"

This poem referred to a powerful weapon that the rogue agents had hidden beneath the ground. It was said to have the power to unleash destruction and bring chaos to the world.

The second poem read:

"In the shadows, a shadow lurks Its eyes on the prize,
its heart a smirk With a smile as sharp as a knife It hides,
waiting for the right time to strike"

This poem referred to a shadowy figure who was still at large, hiding in the shadows and waiting for the right moment to strike. It was clear that there was still a threat to the world, and that the rogue agents had not given up their quest for power and control.

The hero knew that it was up to her to stop this new threat and keep the world safe once and for all. She would always be ready for anything that the world might throw at her, and she was not going to back down until justice had been served.

9 798889 754534

Printed by Libri Plureos GmbH in Hamburg,
Germany